KT-379-303

'It was during Crasner's description of the attack on the security guard that Tim felt a chill running through him. Now he knew how ruthless Crasner was. What would happen to them after his partner arrived and they sorted out the money? How would he react if, as Sue had suggested, his partner didn't come?'

IAN STRACHAN

Bang! Bang!
You're Dead!

Illustrated by Paul Wright

A Magnet Book

To James, who provided the idea
and to Jo and Emma for allowing me
to borrow the time

First published 1988
by Methuen Children's Books Ltd
This Magnet paperback edition first published 1989
by Methuen Children's Books
A Division of the Octopus Group Ltd
Michelin House, 81 Fulham Road, London SW3 6RB

Text copyright © 1988 Ian Strachan
Illustrations copyright © 1988 Paul Wright

Printed and bound in Great Britain by
Cox & Wyman Ltd, Reading, Berks

ISBN 0-416-13192-1

1

'He's here again, Sue!' Tim shouted to his sister above the noise of the tranny which blared out from his bedside table.

Tim was kneeling on his bed peering out through a crack in the curtain at the street below. To anyone else it might have looked a perfectly ordinary damp, cold, winter's morning but not to Tim.

He had no eyes for the newspaper-boy huddled in his brown Balaclava, or for the lone cyclist whose tyres hissed across the black, shiny tarmac. He barely noticed the milkman zigzagging between the doorsteps of the Victorian terraced houses.

Tim's whole attention was focused on the thin man at the bus stop who, despite the unpleasant day, was only wearing jeans, a blue shirt and a shabby jacket with no top coat of any kind. His shoulders were hunched against the cold and his hands thrust so deep into the jacket pockets he was pulling the jacket out of shape.

'Are you coming or what?' Tim shouted.

'In a minute!' Sue shouted back from the bathroom.

Tim couldn't bear the wait. For years he'd been complaining that nothing exciting ever happened to him, the same boring people in the same boring street every day and when something turned up nobody was interested.

He had first spotted the man three, or was it four, days ago. He was certain he'd never seen him before. There was something about him Tim was sure he'd have remembered.

'Furtive,' Tim had said firmly when he first pointed out the mysterious stranger to his sister.

'You got that off the telly,' Sue replied with a toss of her head. 'He's just a bloke waiting for a bus.'

'Then why have I never seen him waiting there before? I know everybody who goes up and down the street.'

'People come and go, you know. They don't have to live here all their lives. New people move in. Or he might just have changed his job, be going to work on a different bus.'

Nothing Tim said would make Sue change her mind. Where Tim saw at least a CIA agent, if not a fugitive from justice, Sue only saw a cold man at a bus stop.

'But he doesn't get on the bus,' Tim announced triumphantly on the second day.

He'd been getting dressed when he heard the bus pull up. He'd expected to see the man climbing

6

aboard but when the bus pulled away and Tim was just about to let the curtain drop back, to his surprise, the thin man suddenly stepped out of the shadows to lean against the bus stop.

'Maybe it was the wrong bus.'

'That's the only bus that goes down here, isn't it?'

'Perhaps he's meeting someone so he's waiting to see if they're on the next bus.'

Sue had an explanation for everything!

But not this! Tim practically fell through the window with excitement. The man was writing something in a notebook.

'Sue! Come here, quick!'

The bathroom door slowly opened and Sue, still brushing her teeth, wandered down the landing as if tomorrow would do.

'Hurry up!' Tim urged but as he spoke Louise Howson came out next door.

'Don't forget my blouse, Mum! I want to wear it down the disco, Saturday!' she shouted so that all the street could hear her, then slammed the front door and tottered off down the road on slender, red high heels.

The second she'd opened the door the man had snapped his notebook shut and stuffed it back into his pocket before easing into the shadows.

Sue was beside Tim. 'What's all the fuss about?'

'The man, the one I've been telling you about, he had a notebook, he was writing things down.'

Sue pushed the curtain wide open so that light

spilled out into the road. 'I can't even see the man let alone any notebook.'

Tim snatched the curtain back across the window. 'He'll see you. He'll know you're watching him. You'll frighten him off.'

'I thought that was what you wanted. You were all for calling the police yesterday.'

Their mother called up the stairs. 'Come on, you two, you'll be late.'

Sue called back. 'We're coming.' Then she turned and hissed under her breath to Tim. 'You shut up about this!'

'I'm off. Don't forget I'll be late tonight, it's Wednesday. I've left the money for Mrs Peebles on the hall table.'

'Right, Mum. Bye.'

'Bye. Bye, Tim.'

Tim called his farewell from the window and watched the thin man as she opened the front door below him. He could see the top of her blonde hair, the shoulders of her shabby but serviceable grey coat and then, as she set off down the street, the green plastic carrier-bag she always carried, with the name of the store where she worked picked out in gold.

She wasn't aware of the man watching her but she knew Tim would be and she turned at the corner of the street to wave before she disappeared.

'Now, get dressed,' Sue said firmly, 'or you'll be going to school without any breakfast.'

'Don't you think we ought to ring the police?'

'And tell them what? There's a man across the road waiting for a bus? Get dressed!'

Twenty minutes later when Tim nipped out of the front door he checked to see if the man was still there but there was no sign of him. It had been exactly the same on the previous days but Tim had that uncomfortable feeling in the back of his neck that convinced him that he was still being watched.

Sue pulled the front door shut and then leaned her weight against it to check it was properly locked. She swung her neatly brushed, gleaming blonde hair back over her shoulder as she looked with distaste at Tim.

'You look like an unmade bed.'

Tim pushed a hand through his tousled hair but ignored the right sock concertina-ed round his ankle and his tie askew.

'Looks aren't everything,' he said airily and stomped off up the pavement.

'A good thing too!' Sue muttered under her breath and rushed to catch up with him.

The man, who watched them go up the street that morning, was back at exactly four o'clock because he knew that was when Tim and Sue met outside the school gate to come home. He also knew that quarter of an hour earlier their next door neighbour, Mrs Howson, would be out walking the dog. As she was the only other person likely to be about at this time of day, the coast was clear.

The thin man glided down the alley between Mrs Howson's and Tim's houses. It ran into the one that went down the backs of all the houses. He'd already checked both ends of that alley because he never knew when that knowledge might come in handy.

For now he was content to give a quick glance at the backs of all the houses. It was dark already and there wasn't a single light showing.

He put his shoulder against the gate that led to Tim's garden, then he slipped through, up the short garden path past the little wooden tool-shed and he was on the back doorstep.

The man slipped on a pair of black leather gloves. One hand held the barrel of a gun. His body was tight with nerves. He was about to break a small pane of glass in the door with the gun when he tried the handle and the door swung open.

He couldn't believe his luck!

A single stride and he was inside, the door shut and he was standing in the kitchen letting his eyes grow accustomed to the dark.

The only sound was the incessant drip, drip, of the tap on to the cold, stainless steel sink.

He checked the luminous dial of his watch then sat down at the kitchen table to wait.

Twenty minutes later Tim and Sue turned into their road. Tim, pleased to be away from school and looking forward to being plonked down in front of the telly, was ahead. Sue was carrying some shopping they'd picked up on the way home.

Suddenly Tim spun round and whipped out a toy gun from his raincoat pocket and aimed it at his sister and fired.

'Bang! Bang! You're dead!' he shouted.

She just looked all superior. 'Mum said you weren't supposed to take guns to school.'

At that exact moment the man got up from the kitchen chair and glided out into the dark hall.

Despite the cold afternoon he was sweating a little. It was nerves not fear that moistened his face. His gloved hand gripped the gun so tightly that it trembled.

Tim startled the man by jumping on to the step so that the orange street light projected his image sharply on to the pane of frosted glass.

The man swallowed and melted back into the shadow by the cellar door as Sue slipped the key into the lock and turned it.

2

'Don't move! I've got a gun.' The man's harsh voice cut through the gloom of the hall.

Tim sensed his elder sister freeze. Sue stood still, her back against the front door she had just slammed shut. The dying rays of the winter sun filtered through the glass.

As Tim's eyes adjusted to the half-light he could just make out the shape of the stranger hunched between the kitchen and cellar doors.

'Walk towards me,' the man ordered. 'Slowly.'

Tim was going to obey but Sue grabbed his hand to stop him. He felt a smear of sweat on her palm so he was suprised how steady her voice sounded. 'You've no right to be here. Who are you? What do you want?'

'Don't you recognise him? It's the man from the bus stop. The one who was watching the house.'

'Shut up and get in the kitchen.'

Neither of them moved.

'Now!'

'We'd better do what he says, Tim.'

Slowly, very slowly, they edged along the narrow strip of hall carpet. When they drew level with the hall table Tim could just make out the neat pile of money Mum had left as usual on a Wednesday for Mrs Peebles.

Beside it was the phone. Maybe he should grab it and ring the police. Clearly the same thought had crossed Sue's mind and she'd decided it wasn't worth the risk because she gripped his hand tightly, practically dragging him past it.

The stranger pressed himself back into the deep shadow by the cellar door to make room for them. Even though Tim couldn't see the man properly he could smell him. He was sweating. Tim was puzzled. The house had been empty all day, it was cold, and outside it was thick with drizzle. If it wasn't sweat from heat then it had to be fear. But what's he got to be frightened of, Tim wondered? He's the one with the gun.

Tim's fingers, deep in his raincoat pocket, closed round the butt of the toy gun. For one heady moment he thought of whipping it out and surprising the man into surrender. But it was only a toy gun and to do that was the simplest way to get himself shot.

The man followed them into the kitchen.

'Take your coats off. You aren't going anywhere.'

Sue took hers off and hung it on the hook behind the door. Tim dropped his damp mac on the kitchen unit. Sue gave him a reproachful glance. Tim thought this seemed an odd time to worry about tidiness.

'How did you get in?' Sue demanded, though her voice wasn't nearly so steady now she was standing close to the man.

'Keep asking questions, don't you? Left the back door unlocked, didn't you? Very careless.' That earned Tim another reproachful look from Sue. She'd asked him to check it before they left for school. 'Sit down.'

He waved them towards the kitchen table. As he did a weak beam of light slid through the half closed slats of the blind and Tim saw it glint on the barrel of his gun.

Tim could not accept that the man had got a gun. It sounded like a TV film. Tim hadn't expected it to be a real gun. But then none of this seemed real. Despite the familiar smells and the insistent drip of the tap Mum had been going to mend for weeks, their kitchen seemed totally alien.

'Sit down!' the man said again.

Tim dropped into a chair beside his sister. Only now did he realise how much his legs had been shaking while he stood up. There was an ache of tension down his calf muscles as if he had just run a race.

'That's better.' The man slid into a chair opposite them. 'There's nothing to be frightened about. If you do as I say, nothing will happen to you.'

The words sounded comforting but when Tim looked up he saw the mean look in the man's thin, grey, bony face and the beads of sweat across his upper lip.

'You know our mother will be back shortly,' Sue lied.

The man's expression changed to scorn. 'You'll have to do better than that. I know where your mum works. Today's Wednesday – late night shopping. She won't be back until gone seven, which gives us the best part of three hours together.'

All the same, the gun trembled slightly in the man's hand. Tim could see Sue'd made him even more nervous and he knew that could be dangerous.

'Like I said, I'm not going to hurt you as long as you shut up and act sensible. For a start, hands on the table, both of you.'

They obeyed. Tim felt a toast crumb, hard and pointed, left over from breakfast. That seemed so far away now as to be in a different lifetime but the time between, the time they'd spent at school, seemed to have disappeared. There was nothing in the world now except this mean, nervous man and the snub, menacing barrel of his gun pointing at them.

Tim was fascinated by the gun. All his favourite TV programmes had guns in and people who fired them at one another. Everything from guided missiles and machine guns to pistols. He longed to own one. He had once held and fired an air pistol belonging to the elder brother of a friend but although it had probably been the greatest thrill of his life, Tim felt it wasn't the same as a proper gun which fired bullets.

This was the closest Tim had ever been to a gun in his life. The strange man who was holding them captive amongst familiar objects made it seem as if they were taking part in a film. Any minute the 'A Team' caption and music would come up and there'd be an ad.

Tim knew he should be afraid and he was, up to a point, but at the same time he couldn't help feeling excited. He wasn't just watching, he was part of the action.

'I used to live here you know.' The man cut through Tim's thoughts.

'When?' Sue asked. Tim could sense there was no way in which Sue was enjoying this.

'Years ago.'

'We've lived here all our lives.' She tilted up her jaw defiantly.

'Oh, this was years ago. Before either of you were born. That's why I've come back.'

'Most people who want to look round their old homes usually knock at the front door and wait to be asked inside. They don't break in.'

The man's free hand shot up. Tim held his breath. He thought the man was going to hit her. The back of his hand hung level with his shoulder for a second, then he relaxed and let it drop back on to the table.

'I've come back,' he went on as if she hadn't spoken, 'to get something that belongs to me, that's all.'

'There's nothing here that belongs to you,' Sue persisted. Tim couldn't understand why she kept pushing her luck.

'Oh, yes, there is, Miss Clever. Hidden away. You wouldn't even know where to look. I've only come to get what's mine. When I've got it I'll go and you'll be none the worse. Fair enough?'

Neither of them answered.

'We'll need some tools. A hammer and chisel. A pickaxe if you've got one.'

'There's one in the shed,' Tim piped up and then screamed, 'Ouch!' as Sue kicked him violently on the shin.

'You're stupid,' she hissed at him.

The man smirked at them. He felt safer now they were arguing. It was while they were together and silent he felt most nervous, not knowing what they were thinking of doing.

Tim rubbed his injured shin. 'What difference does it make? He's only going to take what belongs to him. Where's the harm in that?'

Sue didn't answer. She didn't even look at her brother, she just sniffed and picked at the quick of her fingernail with disgust.

Why couldn't she understand? It seemed so simple to Tim. The man had come back to collect his own property and although he couldn't understand why he'd left it behind in the first place, or why they would need tools to recover it, it seemed perfectly reasonable. Righting a wrong almost. Just like the 'A Team'.

'You, son, you go and get the tools.' Tim stood up to go, anxious to get on with the adventure. 'But remember, your sister's here with me. If you aren't back in five minutes I'll put a bullet through her, understand?'

The man's voice was thin and sharp as steel. The back of Tim's neck felt as if it had just been brushed by a knife.

But Sue seemed unmoved. 'I can't see what good shooting me would do you.'

'Well, if he's gone for help I wouldn't have nothing to lose, would I? And to be honest, putting a bullet through you would give me a great deal of personal satisfaction. So, remember,' he said, turning back to Tim, 'five minutes, or else!'

Tim stumbled on the kitchen step in his hurry to get outside.

'There's something I don't understand,' Sue said.

'Oh, yes. And what's that?'

'You've been watching the house for days and you'd already got in before we got back.'

'So what?'

'Why didn't you take whatever it is you came for and clear out before we came back?'

'Because to get what I want I'm going to have to

make a bit of noise and I'd look a right fool doing that when the place is supposed to be empty, wouldn't I? Anyway, let's just say I like company and leave it at that. Besides, you never know when a hostage or two might come in handy, do you?'

3

Tim stumbled around the dusty shed. Daylight was almost gone. He hadn't been near the shed since the summer. Tim had to climb through a forest of hoe and rake handles to get near the bench.

The bench had been put in by Dad. Mum used the tools sometimes to fix a hinge or repair a fuse, but that was all.

There had to be a hammer or a chisel amongst all these things! Desperately he turned over saws and planes. Something caught at the back of his hand. When he licked it Tim tasted blood but he didn't have time to think about that. The hammer. He found a hammer but he still couldn't find a chisel.

As Tim feverishly turned over the tools he couldn't help imagining his dad handling them. It was stupid he knew because Dad had died while he was still a baby. There was no way Tim could remember him. In fact the only way he knew what his dad had looked like was from an old photograph Mum kept on her dressing-table.

A chisel! His fingers closed round it and he began to clamber back towards the door when he remembered the pickaxe. The five minutes must be nearly up. He went on looking for the pickaxe. Tim felt the chisel slip through his fingers. He heard it hit the wooden floor with a thump and then it rolled away.

Groping about on the floor in the dark, it took ages to extract it from between the prongs of a fork. He had to find the pickaxe now and get back to the house as fast as he could.

He forced the hammer handle through his belt and stuffed the chisel handle into his trouser pocket and at last he caught sight of the rusty head of the pickaxe. Tim grabbed the handle and heaved. There was a thump and clatter as tools fell away and a sharp pain as the handle of one of them hit him in the face just above the eye. But he had the pickaxe and that was all that mattered. Without bothering to close the shed door he ran to the house as fast as he could.

Sue and the man turned to look at him as he almost fell, breathless, into the kitchen.

'Took your time, didn't you? One more minute and "pow".' He eased the lips back from his teeth in a slow leer. 'Did you get everything?'

'This is the pick,' Tim said as he plonked it down on the kitchen tiles. 'And the hammer,' he added pulling it out from his belt by the cold, metal head.

'What about the chisel?'

'I nearly forgot that.' He reached round to his back pocket and put the chisel down on the kitchen table.

'That's a wood chisel, for chiselling wood, stupid! I wanted something to cut through cement and bricks. That's no use.'

'I'm sorry. It's all I could find.'

'Never mind, it'll have to do.'

'Where is whatever it is hidden?'

The man seemed reluctant to answer. He shot a fierce look at Tim and then shrugged. 'I suppose you'll have to know sooner or later. Down in the cellar.'

'There's no light down there,' Sue pointed out.

'I've got a torch,' Tim put in helpfully and this time just managed to move his leg in time as Sue took another swing at him with her shoe and gave him a look that would have withered a tree.

'You run and get it, son,' the man said with a grin.

With Tim returned Sue was asking:

'What are you going to do with us while you're down in the cellar?'

'I could tie you up here, couldn't I?'

Sue's eyes narrowed defiantly. 'You'd need both hands to tie us up so you'd have to put your gun down, wouldn't you? I bet you aren't half so brave without that gun in your hand.'

'I don't think it'll be that difficult. You,' he said looking at Tim, 'find some washing-line or something.'

Not wanting to risk another kick Tim lied. 'I don't know where it is.'

The man laughed out loud but it was a dry laugh with no humour in it. 'Oh, come on, you've been very helpful so far, son. Don't spoil it now.' He raised the barrel of the gun as if he was going to hit Sue across the face. Sue flinched. 'I don't want to get rough.'

Tim hesitated for a split second. He didn't want to anger Sue any more by helping the man but at the same time he couldn't risk her getting hurt.

Tim quickly gave in. 'There's some in the cupboard under the sink.' He found it and as he handed it to the man he couldn't read the expression on Sue's face at all. He just hoped she realised that this time he'd done it for her benefit.

'Sit down again, son.'

'I think you're very brave,' Sue said quietly.

'Why's that?'

'Because as soon as you put that gun down I'll run for the back door to get help and scream as loud as I can.'

'Is that right? Well, Miss Clever, I'm not going to put the gun down, not yet anyway. Not until your brother's tied you up first.'

He opened several drawers until he found the carving knife and cut the length of rope into two, one of which he handed to Tim. 'Tie her up. And make it tight.'

Tim wasn't very good with knots and anyway he didn't want to hurt his sister but at the same time the man was watching closely so he tried to make it look as good as he could. The man was far from satisfied. 'Tighter than that,' he said grabbing the rope and yanking it back so that Sue gasped with pain as it bit into her wrists now behind the back of the chair.

Only when Sue was firmly tied up and Tim had the rope round his wrists did the man put the gun down on the table to finish off the job. The gun was only inches from Tim. He could read the name, 'Walther PX', on the barrel. He longed to get his hands on it. He felt he'd let Sue down badly and he knew that if he had the gun he would be able to make everything right again between them.

Tim felt so miserable he almost didn't notice how uncomfortable he was until the rope began stemming the flow of blood through his veins.

The man stepped back to admire his handiwork. 'Now, you've got a choice. Either you promise not to make a sound or I gag you both and just in case you're in any doubt how that feels. . . .' he pulled a dirty handkerchief from his pocket which he rolled in a ball and thrust towards Sue's face but she drew back as far as she could.

'No, I believe you!' she said quickly. 'We'll keep quiet. Won't we, Tim?' Tim nodded hastily. Just the idea of having that filthy object shoved in his mouth made him feel sick.

The man looked doubtful for a minute. 'One squeak from either of you and you both get it. Understand?' They nodded. He picked up the gun and the tools and left them alone in the kitchen with nothing but the drip, drip, drip of the tap to listen to.

4

'It's not your fault,' Sue hissed at him for the third time.

'I just thought that there was no harm in helping him to get back something that belonged to him in the first place,' Tim whispered.

'Tim!' Sue's voice was heavy with disgust. 'How can you be so thick? Why would anybody break into a house, with a gun and take us prisoner if they'd just called in to collect something which really belonged to them?'

Tim reluctantly agreed. 'I suppose you're right.'

'What I can't understand is why you keep helping the man. When you went to get the torch from upstairs I thought you might have at least tried to telephone for the police.'

'For the same reason I didn't go leaping over the garden wall when I went out to the shed, because I didn't want anything to happen to you.'

'Thanks for that anyway. I suppose we'll just have to wait until he finds what he's come for and hope that he goes away.'

'What *do* you think he's come for then?'

Sue shrugged as much as the rope would allow. 'Search me.'

'That probably comes next,' Tim said with a grin. 'After he's finished knocking the cellar to bits.'

Until Tim spoke the hammering from beneath them had sounded fairly light. But as the pickaxe bit deeply into the concrete floor, the whole house seemed to vibrate.

'While he's making that racket we could try and get these ropes off,' Sue suggested. 'If we can both get away together then nobody will get hurt.'

'I've been trying but mine are too tight.'

'Maybe if we shuffled the chairs back to back we could untie each other.'

As the man hadn't bothered to tie their feet it was quite easy to manouevre themselves but because there was only the floor between them and the man, they had to do it as quietly as possible and it was some time before Tim's fingers were struggling with Sue's knots. Not only was the knot behind him, so that he could only feel his way round it, but his fingers couldn't get a grip because they kept slipping off the washing-line's plastic coating. Just when he thought he'd got hold of the loose end and it was moving, he lost his grip and had to start all over again. Very quickly his arms and fingers were aching and he had to give up.

'They're too tight for me,' he reluctantly admitted.

'Let me try.'

Tim felt Sue's slim, bony fingers probing and pulling at the knot.

'Keep still!' Sue complained. 'I'd almost got it then.'

'Sorry. Listen!'

'What?'

'The hammering, it's stopped.'

'Too right it has!' They both turned to see the man, hot and dusty, standing in the doorway watching them. 'What do you two think you're doing? Playing bookends?'

He swung Tim's chair round so fast that if Tim hadn't been tied to it he would have fallen off and he ended up facing Sue.

'Well, if you've got what you came for perhaps you'll untie us before you go,' Sue suggested.

The man tucked his thumb into his belt next to where the gun was lodged. 'That's the whole point, duck. I haven't.'

Sue looked surprised. 'You haven't?'

The man shook his head slowly, watching her carefully. 'No, because somebody got there before me, didn't they?'

She clearly didn't know what the man was talking about. 'I wouldn't know.'

'Somebody's dug up that floor and taken what we put under there.'

A bang at the back door made them all three jump. It was followed by a woman's voice. 'Are you all right, chuck?'

'Who's that?' the man whispered.

'Our next door neighbour, Mrs Howson. She probably heard you banging about in the cellar.'

'Susan, are you there, chuck?'

'She knows we're in here. She often comes round when Mum's out to see we're all right.'

'Get rid of her,' the man hissed and Tim could see he was trembling.

'I can't just shout to her. I'll have to answer the door otherwise she'll know there's something wrong won't she?'

'All right.' The man grabbed the knife and in one movement hacked through the rope. She winced with pain and rubbed her wrists where the rope had left angry, red marks.

There was another knock at the door. Louder and more insistent. 'Susan! Are you two all right in there?'

'Remember,' the man spat out the words, 'he's with me.' With no effort he picked Tim up still seated on the kitchen chair. 'If you foul things up, he gets it!'

Tim was dumped in the hall where they could both hear what Sue was doing and saying. Just in case Tim forgot how important it was, he suddenly felt the cold metal of the gun barrel pressed against his neck like a hard, icy finger.

'Hello, Mrs Howson.'

'I've been knocking and knocking. I was that worried. What are you doing in there? What was all that banging about?'

There was a pause. Tim wondered what on earth Sue was going to say. He just hoped she got it right.

'Oh, I'm sorry about that. It was Tim doing some woodwork in the cellar.'

Typical, Tim thought, blame me! But for once he didn't mind.

'Woodwork? I thought the whole house was coming down. I said to Stan, I'll have to go and see they're all right.'

'We're fine, thanks, Mrs Howson.'

'Oh, well, if you're sure. Woodwork you say? Mmm, I saw young Tim out in the shed earlier.'

Nosy devil, Tim thought. Why hadn't she been watching when the man broke in in the first place, then we wouldn't be in this mess?

'Well, if you're sure it's all right?' Mrs Howson seemed uncertain.

'Yes, fine,' Sue insisted.

Why doesn't she go? Tim kept asking himself as the gun kept pressing harder and harder against his neck.

'Oh, I've just thought, I lent your mum a pair of dressmaking scissors. Only I need them for a blouse I'm making for our Louise. I think I saw them in the sitting-room yesterday.'

Tim felt the barrel dig into his neck as Mrs Howson's footsteps came towards the kitchen door and the man froze. Any second she would come round the door and see them. Tim stopped breathing and braced himself for the shot he felt would come in the next second.

'Aren't these the scissors?' Sue's voice sounded strained and high pitched. Even as she spoke Tim saw the door move as her meaty hand grasped its edge. Another beat and she would have been in the hall.

'Oh, yes, chuck. They're the ones.' Tim sighed with relief as he felt the man behind him relax very slightly while they watched her hand disappear from view. 'I'm lost without them and Louise is set on wearing this blouse to the disco on Saturday. Two days! I ask you? I said to her, you might have given me a bit of warning.'

Tim wanted to scream out, 'Go away, you silly old bag!' at the top of his voice. He couldn't bear the waiting while she burbled along.

'Well, if you're sure you're all right.' Her footsteps moved away towards the back door then she stopped again. 'Where's Timmy now?'

He hated it when she called him Timmy but never more so than now. He suspected that any second she was going to come looking for him.

'Up in his room putting up the bookcase.'

'Bookcase?'

'Yes, that's what he was making down in the cellar.' Tim could have hugged his sister.

'Oh, I see. Well, I must go. I've got tea to get yet.' There was another pause. You could almost hear the rusty cogs in her brain turning. The trouble was it was so agonisingly slow. Each of these pauses seemed like a lifetime to Tim. Then at last she

34

spoke. 'What would Timmy want with a bookcase? I thought telly was more in his line. I've never seen him with a book in his hand in his life.'

'That's true,' Sue admitted, 'well, perhaps he's turning over a new leaf.'

'Mind you our Louise is one for a good read.'

Oh, no! She's off again.

'She's reading *Lace* at the moment. She says it's. . . .'

'I've just remembered,' Sue cut in, 'I left the bath running.'

'Oh, you see to it, chuck. I'll see myself out. Just knock if you need me.'

'I will,' Sue shouted as she rounded the door and almost fell over Tim in the hall. She kept herself upright with a hand on either wall until they heard the back door shut then she fell in a heap on the floor like a puppet whose strings had been cut and began to sob loudly, mostly from relief that that part of the ordeal was over.

5

'I can't drink with my arms tied up,' Tim protested. Without a word the man hacked through the rope and Tim was free to move except for the painful stiffness in his arms.

They were back in the kitchen celebrating with a cup of coffee which the man had made. Opposite Tim, Sue sat red-eyed and still shaking.

'You might as well be free. We've got nearly an hour to wait now.' The man had taken his coffee over to the sink and was sitting on the draining-board.

'How do you mean?' Tim always wanted to know everything.

'Because he's got a friend coming,' Sue put in before the man had chance to answer.

Instantly his face changed from relaxed to suspicious. 'How do you know that? Who's been talking?'

'Only you.' Sue looked smug at the man's discomfort. 'Just before Mrs Howson knocked on the door you said that somebody else must have dug up the cellar floor before you because what "we put under there" wasn't there any more. I guessed straight away that there was somebody else involved and although you'd arranged to meet them here you wouldn't mind having whatever was hidden all to yourself. I bet if you'd found what you were looking for you'd be gone by now. You wouldn't be waiting for anyone.'

'That's not true. We were partners. Fifty-fifty, that's what we agreed.'

'But you were still happy to take the lot if you could get your hands on it. Only thing is, it looks as if he's beaten you to it.' Tim could see that she was taunting him. Perhaps trying to get her own back for the ordeal he'd put her through.

'Shut up!'

Tim couldn't help asking. 'What was hidden down there?'

'Money. About two million pounds.'

'Two million pounds? Buried in our cellar and we knew nothing about it?' Tim couldn't believe his ears particularly when he thought how hard Mum had to work for every penny she brought home. And here they'd been living on top of a fortune.

'Don't get excited, Tim. It wasn't money you could spend. It was stolen wasn't it?' The man hesitated only briefly before giving a curt nod. 'So what use would it be to anyone? The second anyone spent one of those bank notes the numbers would be recognised and the police would be there in a flash.'

'How do you know so much about it?' Tim was puzzled.

'A few days ago it was in all the papers, wasn't it?' She turned towards the man who nodded again but still didn't speak. 'When I first saw you I thought I recognised you but I couldn't think from where, I thought it was seeing you at the bus stop but then I remembered this story about somebody escaping from prison who'd been involved in a two-million-pound bank robbery. They never recovered the money.'

'Escaped prisoner?' Tim had to be sure he'd heard right because if he had this was turning out to be the best adventure he'd ever had.

'That's right, son.' The man recognised hero worship when he heard it and grinned smugly.

'That's fantastic!'

'Oh, Tim, come on! He's a crook not captain of the England football team.'

Tim wasn't listening to her. 'How did you do it?'

'It wasn't that difficult.' The man was trying to sound modest. 'You need a plan that's all. If you've got a good plan and you're prepared to improvise if things change, you can't fail. They were taking me to hospital for an operation, nothing serious, and when I'd been there before for observation I'd noticed a back staircase with a door to it that was always locked. One of the porters used it to take out sacks of rubbish. He wasn't supposed to, but he was lazy and he had a key so why not? He also liked a

38

drink and one night when he'd had a few I borrowed the key off him, made an impression of it in my soap, then gave it him back. By the time I went back for the op., I'd made myself a key in the prison workshop that took me all the way to the outside world.'

'That's amazing!' Tim's mouth was so wide open with admiration his chin was almost on the table.

Sue snorted her disgust. 'And now he's come round here to collect two million pounds he can't spend.'

'That's where you're wrong, Miss Clever. That money was laundered before it was hid.'

'Laundered?' Tim had visions of it going round in a washing machine until he remembered the time Mum had left a five pound note in her jeans pocket. There was very little of the note left and all the other washing had soggy blobs of paper clinging to it.

'All the cops and robbers you watch on telly, Tim, and you don't know what laundered means!' Sue's voice was heavy with scorn. 'Straight after the robbery you change the notes you've stolen for different ones and the ones you keep can't be traced by the numbers any more.'

Tim looked blank. 'How do you do that?' It was Sue's turn to look baffled now.

'There are all kinds of ways. If you're quick you can lend it someone and then when they pay you back they give you new notes. But most of it goes out of the country. There are people who'll do it for you, at a price.'

39

'If I remember right,' Sue went on, 'this bright spark,' she jerked her thumb at the man, 'was caught by the police with some of the original notes on him.'

'Yes, well, I was going to change them, wasn't I? Anyway, I hadn't got much on me.'

'Enough to tie you in with the robbery and put .you away in prison.'

'They just got lucky. I was on my way to change about five hundred quid and they stopped me for speeding. They searched the car and found the money.'

'You see, Tim, he hadn't even got the sense to drive properly.'

But Tim wasn't listening to Sue. He was so busy thinking about what you could do with two million pounds that he'd even forgotten that the money was stolen and the man had no right to it at all. Tim's head was so full of images of Robin Hood that he also forgot that this man had no intention of giving it to anyone, let alone the poor. He had no intention of sharing the money with his partner even if he could get away with it.

'How long have you been on the run?' Tim asked.

'Six days.'

'It shouldn't be long before they catch you then.'

'Listen,' he glowered at Sue, 'if you don't shut your mouth I'll shut it for you.'

Sue wasn't put off by his threat. 'They caught you last time,' she pointed out.

'Only because we were still sorting out the money. We'd arranged to split up until that was done, let things cool off. Then we were going to take just enough to get us out of the country, leave the rest buried here, and come back when it was all forgotten. My partner and me, we had got that hole ready for the money when they caught me.'

The shrill bell of the telephone cut through the house like a knife. All three froze. Both Sue and Tim knew exactly who it was but this time Tim caught Sue's warning look and kept his mouth shut.

The phone kept on ringing. In the totally silent house it sounded terribly loud. Tim couldn't bear the sound. Normally he would be the first to answer because he was always frightened that it would stop ringing before he could get to it and then he would never know who was ringing. Even though he knew perfectly well that it was Mum, it still had the same effect on him.

'We'd better answer it,' Sue suggested when it kept on ringing. She began to get up but the man waved her back to her chair with his gun.

'Leave it!' he said. 'If you touch that phone I'll rip it out of the wall.'

6

Hours seemed to pass with the phone ringing. Tim wondered what Mum must be thinking when they didn't answer. She probably wasn't in the least bit worried. She knew they were capable of looking after themselves. On Wednesdays they not only prepared supper but also cooked it ready for her return. As suddenly as it had started the phone stopped.

In the silence which followed Tim found himself wishing, briefly, that Mum was there and that the man wasn't. But then he thought about the tales he'd be able to tell his mates. The fact that it was a tale he might not live to tell hadn't crossed his mind.

As they all three relaxed, Sue asked the man quietly, 'What happened to your partner?'

'What's it to you?' he snapped back.

'I was only wondering.'

'He's been living in Spain ever since. The English police can't touch him there even if they have any proof he was part of the robbery – which they haven't.'

Sue thought about that for a moment. 'So, all the time you've been rotting in prison he's been lying in the sun on the Costa Packet?'

'Don't start again with the "aggro"!' he warned her.

'And he's risking coming here tonight to meet you?'

'Course he is. We're partners, aren't we?'

'But if he comes back and gets caught with you then you'll both end up in jail.'

The donkey bray of a police siren cut through the silence of the night.

'That's probably them now,' Sue cut in with a grin.

'Shut up.' The man left the kitchen and rushed down the hall towards the front door. The second he was out of the room Sue made a dash for the back door beckoning Tim to follow. 'Now's our chance!'

Sue yanked at the handle only to discover he must have bolted the door some time after Mrs Howson had left.

'Nice try!' The man leant against the doorpost watching them. Their footsteps had brought him back.

Sue's shoulders slumped in despair as the noise of the siren faded into the darkness.

'If I can't trust you two I can always tie you up again,' he threatened.

'You can't blame us for trying,' Sue pointed out defiantly.

'Maybe not,' he replied. 'But I don't have to like it, do I? And I certainly don't have to give you another chance.' He glanced at his watch. 'We've got another half-hour to wait, let's try and keep it pleasant, eh?'

Sue and Tim slumped back into their chairs. Secretly Tim wasn't all that disappointed that the escape attempt had failed. Having got this far he wanted to see it through to the end.

The trouble was that although Tim knew that this man was an escaped convict, which meant he was a criminal, Tim couldn't help having a sneaking admiration for him. Apart from anything else he'd beaten the system. Of course he had got caught but the police had never recovered the money and now the man had succeeded in getting away.

Tim was confused. He knew he shouldn't be thinking this way but he wasn't the only one these days to admire people who got away with things.

Take Mum for example. He knew for a fact that she had her overtime paid to her in cash so that the tax man never got to hear of it. He also knew that when Gran had had a bit of a fire she'd claimed far more off the insurance than she'd really lost.

Tim knew this because they'd both boasted openly about it, about how they'd beaten the system. He'd even heard people saying about a big gold robbery that the crooks had been so cheeky they deserved to get away with it. And besides, just like his Gran, the company that lost the gold had been insured so nobody really lost in the end, did they?

Tim could easily push the simple idea that stealing was stealing, whichever way you looked at it, right to the back of his mind.

'Were you all over the papers?' he asked.

The man had the grace to blush slightly but he still felt round in the back pocket of his jeans and pulled out a dog-eared collection of newspaper clippings. 'Just a bit,' he said modestly as he pushed them across to Tim.

Tim unfolded the cuttings and spread them out on the table in front of him pressing them straight with the flat of his palms. It might have been the kind of collection anyone else would have kept of their favourite footballer's latest match.

'DARING ESCAPE', 'PRISONER FLEES HOSPITAL' were typical of the headlines. Most of the articles concentrated on the details of how Bob Crasner had escaped from the hospital. Most of the photographs were taken at least eight years ago when Crasner was arrested and Tim couldn't recognise him as the man standing in their kitchen.

Some of the articles described the robbery as 'daring' and 'cheeky'.

Sue, who hadn't been paying much attention, pulled one of the articles across the table and began to read from it.

'Fifty-seven year old Tom Cannon, father of two, the security guard who got severely beaten during the robbery, has for the past eight years been in a coma as a result of the injuries he sustained.'

Crasner snatched the cutting out of her hand. It ripped as she held on to part of it. He grabbed that bit too and stuffed it deep into his pocket.

'What they want to drag that up for?' Crasner snapped. 'Water under the bridge that is.'

'Not to him,' Sue said quietly. 'Nor to his wife and children.'

'Shouldn't have got in the way, should he? Wanted to be a hero, didn't he?' Crasner bit his bottom lip then went on, not looking at Sue or Tim. 'There was only him between us and the money. I mean we could actually see the stuff! All that planning, for months, and there it was, ripe for the taking.' Crasner's eyes were sparkling. 'We'd slipped over the back wall spot on time when the gate men were changing over. They were too busy signing on and off to notice us. Across the yard and in through the back door. Opened up like a sardine tin, that did. We'd been checking everybody's movements for weeks. Got it all down to a fine art. We hid in this broom cupboard for ten minutes while the guard went past like he did every night. You could see all this from the roof of the building opposite. Night after night we were up there watching in the freezing cold. We knew we had to lose ten minutes, so we hid, that way the guard would be nowhere near when we went for the money.'

Tim had been listening, fascinated.

'So what went wrong?' It was Sue who asked the question and Tim could tell from her tone that she wasn't nearly as impressed by the story.

Crasner hit the table with his hand so suddenly that they both jumped back in their seats. 'He stopped to go to the loo! Probably had an extra cup of tea or something, I don't know, anyway that night instead of doing his rounds spot on time, as he had for weeks, he was late. Walked in on us just as we were going to lift the money. He should have been at the other end of the building by then but here he was right in our way.'

'And you beat him up?'

'That was his own fault.'

Even Tim couldn't stomach that. 'How could it have been his fault?' Tim felt bitter that the man he'd been building up as a hero should have done such a thing.

'Got in the way, didn't he? I mean he could have cleared off, turned a blind eye. I mean it wasn't as if he was supposed to be in that part of the building at the time. But no, he wanted to make a name for himself. Wanted to be a hero. Not only was he in the way and quite ready to have a go but his finger was on the alarm. I had to stop him. You can see that, can't you?' They both stayed silent but Crasner didn't notice. He was too busy reliving that moment.

'I hit him, hard, on the back of the head with this

47

pickaxe handle I was carrying. He went down like a sack of potatoes. But he didn't stay still even then. He was still fumbling about for his alarm. So I hit him again and again and again.'

Crasner's voice had risen to a shout but now it stopped abruptly and the echo died away in the corners of the room.

'He didn't move again after that,' Crasner added, looking at the floor in front of him as if the body might still be there. Crasner glanced up, caught the horrified look on both their faces and tried to justify himself. 'It was his own fault. Trying to make a name for himself, trying to be a hero.'

Tim couldn't think of anything to say but in that moment he realised that all the bodies he'd seen on television hadn't been real ones, they'd been actors, and they hadn't been hurt by anything. When the cameras stopped turning they'd got up and gone home, unlike the security guard.

Crasner shook his head. 'Trying to be a hero!'

There was silence for a few seconds and then Sue said, almost in a whisper, 'Seems to me he was.'

7

It was during Crasner's description of the attack on the security guard that Tim felt a chill running through him. Now he knew how ruthless Crasner was. What would happen to them after his partner arrived and they'd sorted out the money? How would he react if, as Sue had suggested, his partner didn't come?

Either way he and Sue had seen Crasner, knew he was an escaped prisoner. He must know that the second he left the house they would ring the police.

As he watched Crasner sulkily gathering up the press cuttings Tim wondered how far Crasner would go to stop them giving him away to the police? Tim could not forget Crasner's brutal attack on the security guard and shivers shot down his spine.

There was one newspaper cutting, half buried beneath the others, that caught Tim's eye just as Crasner was about to pick it up. On this one there was not only Crasner's picture but another man as well. 'Who's that?' At first Tim thought it might be the security guard.

'My partner.'

'He looks a lot older than you,' Tim said as he pulled the picture towards him to get a better look at it. Tim felt there was something vaguely familiar about the other face. He couldn't think where he'd seen it though. Perhaps he'd seen it with half an eye on the television news?

'Mine's an old photo,' Crasner explained. 'That's a new one. Taken in Spain.'

'So the police know where he is?'

'Have done all the time.'

'Then why don't they arrest him?' Sue asked.

'He hasn't committed any crime there.'

'I meant the British police.'

'For one thing they've no evidence against him and, even if they had, they couldn't get him out of Spain.'

Sue thought about that for a moment. 'But you've just told us he was involved.'

Crasner tried to pretend that he knew that all the time but it was easy to see from the look on his face that he hadn't really. 'They'd still have to find the evidence to make it stick.'

'Both of you caught with two million pounds would be enough though, wouldn't it?'

Tim wished Sue would shut up. Didn't she realise that her attitude just made their chances of escaping after Crasner and his partner had left even more unlikely?

'I tell you one thing,' Crasner obviously wanted

to change the subject too, 'I need some different things to wear. These are the same things I left the hospital in and they'll make me easy to spot.'

'There isn't anything,' said Sue.

'There must be something,' he protested.

Tim shook his head. 'There's only Mum, Sue and me. There aren't any men's clothes. Dad died just before I was born.'

Crasner opened his mouth to speak then thought better of it.

Then Tim suddenly had a brain wave. 'What about one of Mum's coats?'

'Tim!' Sue didn't bother to kick him this time but the expression on her face and in her voice were both heavy with meaning.

But Tim wasn't going to be stopped. He was only too eager to do anything he could to help Crasner get out of the house as quickly as possible.

'Better than nothing I suppose,' Crasner grudgingly admitted. 'Let's go and have a look, see what there is. You lead the way.'

Sue glared at Tim then got up and walked towards the stairs. Tim followed. As they walked down the hall he was aware of Crasner keeping the gun at the ready.

As they passed the front door Crasner took the opportunity of dropping the catch on the Yale lock and slipping on the safety chain just in case they had any ideas of making a dash for it that way.

Tim couldn't help thinking that it seemed hours.

since they had come through the door, but when he glanced at his watch he realised it was only about three quarters of an hour. And there was still quarter of an hour to go before Crasner's partner was due to arrive.

Sue switched on the lights upstairs. 'This is Mum's room.'

Tim had often been in there before but tonight, with Crasner and his gun held firmly in his hand, it seemed so weird. Home was somewhere you came to when things went wrong. Somewhere you always felt safe. But not any more. Tim didn't think he'd ever feel safe here, ever again.

Crasner pulled open the wardrobe door with his free hand.

'Don't . . .' Susan began and then broke off.

It was obvious to Tim that she felt it was wrong that this complete stranger should go through Mum's things when she wasn't there. They'd always respected each other's privacy. None of them would have dreamt of prying in each other's rooms.

'Sit down on the bed and shut up. There's a mirror on the inside of this door so I can still see what you're doing even if I've got my back to you.'

Tim and Sue sat side by side on the bed. There was a scent of Mum in the room that brought a lump to Tim's throat. If only she was here now! He knew that she wouldn't be able to do anything any more than they could but at least they would all have been together.

The coathangers squealed in protest as Crasner roughly pushed them aside, rejecting garment after garment.

Tim's eyes wandered round the room that seemed so familiar and yet so strange, then suddenly he froze.

'This might do at a pinch,' Crasner said pulling an old, dark blue gabardine mackintosh off its hanger. At least it was something Mum hadn't worn for years and probably wouldn't even miss, Tim thought, but his mind was elsewhere.

'Can I have another look at those newspaper cuttings?'

Crasner was busy trying on the coat watching himself and them in the mirror. 'What? Yeah, sure.'

He pulled the cuttings out of his pocket and threw them down on the green bedcover beside Tim.

Tim knew only too well which one he was looking for. When he found it he got up and walked over to Mum's dressing-table.

Crasner, the coat half-on and half-off spun round, the gun at the ready. 'What are you up to? Sit down.'

But Tim took no notice.

'I said, sit down.' Crasner was pointing the gun straight at Tim. His trigger finger twitched slightly.

'Do as he says, Tim,' Sue pleaded.

Tim wasn't listening. He wasn't being brave, he couldn't hear a word either of them was saying for the words that were swirling round and round in his head until they made him feel dizzy.

'I'll give you two seconds,' Crasner threatened.

Tim held up the cutting beside the photograph on Mum's dressing-table and in a flash he knew why the man in the newspaper cutting had seemed familiar. They were the same man.

Tim felt the room sway then he crashed to the floor in a faint.

8

When Tim came round he was lying on the bed still clutching the newspaper cutting. Sue had loosened his collar and was peering anxiously at him. Even Crasner, who was standing at the end of the bed, looked concerned.

'What you want to go and do a thing like that for, son? Scared the daylights out of us.'

'Sue, look at this.' He waved the cutting at her. 'It's Dad. Dad was his partner in the robbery. He isn't dead at all. He's living in Spain.'

Sue nodded. 'I know.'

'Do you mean you've always known?' Despite being weak Tim was very angry at the thought that she had kept this secret from him for years.

'No. I began to put two and two together downstairs. As soon as he said he used to live here I was suspicious. This house used to belong to Gran until we moved in, didn't it?' Tim nodded, he'd forgotten that. 'And anyway when people move out they take things with them not hide them. And yet you seemed to know the house so well. You seemed familiar with the layout.' She turned to look at Crasner for a moment and then turned back to Tim. 'I worked out he must have been here before even if he didn't live here.'

'Oh, I've been here,' Crasner said. 'I used to sleep in that little room above the front door.'

'That's my room.' Tim sat up.

'You weren't even born then. Your mum was carrying you last time I come.'

'I've never seen you before in my life. You couldn't have stayed here,' Sue protested.

'Oh, yes, I have,' Crasner grinned. 'You were only little then. Your dad slipped me in after you'd gone to bed and I was always gone before you woke up. Your mum didn't like it though.'

'I can't say I blame her,' Sue muttered but Crasner wasn't listening.

'We used to come back frozen from keeping watch on top of that building. We spent hours sitting in the kitchen planning how we were going to do the job.'

Things were moving too quickly for Tim. The house was beginning to feel unfamiliar again but in a totally different way now he knew that Crasner had been there long before he was born. The whole thing was becoming more fantastic by the second.

'But why didn't Mum ever tell us any of this?' Tim demanded. 'And why did she lie about him being dead?'

'To protect us. She obviously knew what he'd

done and she wasn't very proud of it. Rather than tell us, as he'd cleared off to Spain anyway, she told us he was dead. After all he wasn't here, so for her he might just as well have been.'

'And we believed her.'

'I remember asking her once where he was buried.'

'What did she say?'

'She didn't. She just changed the subject. So then I asked Gran. She just said I shouldn't bother my head with such things and I forgot all about it after that. Would you like a glass of water, Tim? You still look very pale.'

Tim nodded. 'Yes, please.'

'Is it all right if I get him one from the bathroom?'

'Yes, but don't try anything.'

'What could I do in the bathroom? Flush myself out of the house?' She flounced out of the room and Tim had to laugh at her cheek, in spite of the way he felt, but Crasner just scowled and went back to trying on the raincoat.

Sue came back with the glass of water as Crasner was stuffing the other clothes back in the wardrobe.

'Don't do that to Mum's clothes,' she told him. 'Mum has to work hard to pay for those. We don't just steal everything we need.'

Tim was just taking a sip of water when a loud bang at the front door nearly made him choke.

'What the hell's that?' said Crasner looking at his watch. 'It's only ten to. Maybe he's early. Where are you going?'

The last was to Tim, who had thrust the glass back at Sue, rolled off the bed and was heading for the landing.

'I'll be able to see if it's Dad from my bedroom window. It looks right down on the front door.'

Before Crasner could protest, Tim was heading for his own bedroom and by the time Crasner and Sue joined him all they could see was his legs. He'd opened the window and leant right out to get a good view.

A woman's voice drifted up through the darkness from the front step. 'Hello, Tim, I've turned up again, like a bad penny.'

Tim pulled his head back inside. The disappointment was written all over his face.

'Is it your Mum?'

'No,' said Sue. 'It's Mrs Peebles.'

'Not another nosy neighbour.'

'No, she comes every Wednesday to collect the money.'

'Money? What money?'

'I told you Mum has to work hard to pay for her clothes, didn't I? Most of them she orders from a catalogue Mrs Peebles brings round. Then she pays for them bit by bit each week until she's paid it off, then she orders something else.'

'Are you coming down or not?' Mrs Peebles' voice drifted up through the darkness.

'We'll have to pay her or she'll think something's very odd. Mum's never missed a week. Even when

we go on holiday she always leaves the money next door.'

'This house is like Waterloo Station.' Crasner grumbled.

'The money's on the hall table.'

'All right then. But he stays up here with me. So no funny business. Understand?'

Sue nodded and left. They both listened. They heard her go downstairs then they heard the chain come off and the lock being opened.

'Freezing out here tonight, love.'

'It is cold, isn't it.'

'Have you got the right money? Only I'm a bit short of change tonight. Everyone's been giving me notes.'

'I think it's right. You'd better check it.'

There was a pause and a chink of coins as Mrs Peebles' cold fingers fumbled through them.

'Get on with it, woman,' Crasner hissed through clenched teeth.

Tim thought it odd that a harmless old woman like Mrs Peebles could make a man like Crasner so jumpy.

'Yes, dear, that's right. Oh, dear!'

Tim couldn't believe his ears. Mrs Peebles had dropped the lot on the front step. They could hear coins rolling all over the place. Some flopped on the step but others rolled down the steps on to the pavement and into the gutter.

'What's she doing now?'

'Picking it up. She'll stick at it right up to the last penny. Sometimes it takes hours. We go through this every week with her. Hardly a week goes by without she drops some of the money.'

'Not tonight.'

'You're thinking about Dad?'

'If he comes while she's hanging about on the steps he'll just go away.'

Crasner's voice was tense and Tim could see a thin knot of blue vein throbbing in his forehead.

'Have you got it all now, Mrs Peebles?' Sue's voice drifted up to the open window.

'Let's just count it again, dear.' There was a long pause during which Crasner held his breath. 'There's five pence short. You count it and check.'

'Oh, no!' sighed Crasner.

'I'll take your word for it, Mrs Peebles. Now why don't you put that money away while it's safe and we'll look for the five pence.'

'What a good idea,' said Mrs Peebles, just as if she would never have thought of it for herself.

'If she drops it again now,' muttered Crasner, 'I'll put a bullet through her, so help me!'

Tim believed he would too. But fortunately the cash was safely stowed away for the next thing they heard was Mrs Peebles saying, 'I wonder where that other five pence has gone.'

'Five pence! The woman is ruining my chance of getting my hands on a million pounds for five pence! I can't believe this is happening.' He slapped his forehead with the palm of his hand. Then he fumbled in his pocket and brought out a pile of change. 'Take her this. Give it to her, all of it. Anything, but get rid of her!'

Crasner was so worked up about Mrs Peebles he'd clearly forgotten that Tim was his hostage.

Tim's heart began to beat fast as he stretched out to take the coins. He knew that the moment he reached the bottom of the stairs Sue would grab him, pull him out into the street and they would be free. His fingers closed over the coins, hot from Crasner's pocket and greasy from his sweating palm, when Mrs Peebles spoke again.

'Here it is. It was caught in my coat cuff! Aren't I a silly billy? Sorry to waste your time, love. See you next week.'

She was off down the road. Tim hardly noticed and wasn't aware that with her went their last chance to escape from Crasner. A new and thrilling idea was starting to take shape.

9

'I don't care what you say, Sue, I'm going with Dad when he leaves here.' Tim's voice rang out across the kitchen.

There was the hint of a smile on Crasner's lips but Sue not only looked upset but very angry. 'Just like that, after all Mum's done for us? She's worked herself into the ground bringing us up, keeping this place together and going out to work. Now you want to walk out on her with the man who left her in the lurch.'

'Dad had to go.'

'Not if he hadn't done anything wrong. He could have worked for a living like everyone else. Scrimped and saved for what he wanted just like Mum's had to ever since he left.'

'Maybe he got fed up with all the scrimping and saving. I have. Always having to make do. Look how long I've had to wait for a new bike. All the other kids have got bikes. Look at me, I haven't even learnt to ride yet. I'm the only kid in our class that can't ride a bike. Every Christmas and birthday I ask for a bike and Mum comes up with the same old answer, "We can't afford it." Well, I'm sick of that. I want a bike and I want it now.'

Sue looked pityingly at Tim. 'So you're going to run off with a man you've never met for that?'

'He's my dad.'

'That's something he seems to have forgotten, isn't it. Otherwise why hasn't he been in touch until now?'

'Maybe he writes to Mum every week.'

'Don't talk wet, Tim!'

'He could for all we know. Mum lied to us about his being dead when he was alive all the time, perhaps she's hidden the letters.'

'I doubt that,' Sue said firmly, 'but there's one thing for sure.'

'Oh, yes, and what's that?'

'He certainly hasn't been sending us money or we wouldn't have been living from hand to mouth the way we have. Mum turning collars on your shirts to make them last and getting to the butcher late on Saturday so his prices are dropping on meat he can't put back in the freezer.' Sue's face was red with anger as she leant forward across the table to make her point.

Tim hated arguments at the best of times and he hated them with Sue worst of all. Maybe because of Mum being out at work and so busy when she got home, they'd grown up closer than most brothers and sisters. They fell out over stupid things like who has the bathroom first in the morning but those arguments flared up quickly and disappeared within seconds. Mostly they got along very well. Tim couldn't remember when they'd ever had a disagreement like this and it made his stomach burn so much he felt sick. But he still couldn't give up. It was as if something inside him was driving him on, something he could no longer control.

Crasner, who'd been watching them both, came and sat at the end of the table between them. His voice was oily. 'How do you know your dad didn't offer to take your mum with him when he went to Spain?'

'What if he did?' Sue retorted.

'Well, if he did and she refused, then it isn't his fault she's had a hard time making ends meet here, is it?' Crasner pointed out.

'He didn't tell you he was going to Spain, did he?' Sue snapped back.

Crasner went red and blustered, 'Yes he did.' Even Tim could see he was lying. 'Anyway, I told you, we'd arranged to split up.'

'So that he could get clean away with the money while the police picked you up.'

Crasner slapped his hand down on the table. 'It wasn't like that.'

'Oh no?' Sue was very much in control now. It was her turn to goad Crasner. 'I wonder if it was just accident the police got on to you.'

'How do you mean?' Crasner's eyes narrowed and Tim could feel the hatred flowing out of him.

'Maybe he tipped them off and the driving incident was just an excuse.'

Even Tim felt this was going too far and he leapt to his father's defence. 'Dad wouldn't grass. He wouldn't double-cross anyone.'

'How do you know? You've never met him, you know nothing about him.'

'Nor do you then.'

'So we can only judge him by his actions, agreed?' Sue waited for Tim to nod before she went on. 'He double-crossed Mum, so why shouldn't he double-cross his partner. After all, if he got away with it he stood to gain a million pounds because I reckon he'd already got one million with him. How else could he have lived in Spain all this time?'

'He didn't take the money with him!' Crasner almost shouted. Tim couldn't help wondering if Crasner was getting so worked up because he was beginning to suspect that what Sue was saying was true.

'You couldn't find it in the cellar,' Sue said triumphantly.

'Even if he did, he'd still give me my share.'

'If he's still got it.'

'Shut up! Just shut up. You know it all, don't you?' He waved the gun menacingly at her. 'It wouldn't be worth his while to cross me, I tell you that!'

66

Sue shrugged and let the matter drop. There was silence for a few seconds. Sue picked at her fingernail while Crasner glared at her.

Then Tim said very quietly. 'I'm still going with Dad when he comes.'

'If,' Sue cut in.

'When,' Tim repeated more firmly.

'Why? Just tell me why.'

'What's it to you?'

'Nothing, but I'd like to be able to tell Mum, that's all and I certainly can't work it out for myself.'

Up to that moment Tim had only thought of going with his dad. He hadn't considered leaving his mum behind. Suddenly there was a bleak feeling but he pushed it aside irritably. 'Anything would be more exciting than being here.'

'Do you call this exciting?' She waved a hand towards Crasner and his gun. 'Do you call being arrested and sent to prison exciting?'

'Dad hasn't been sent to prison.'

'Not yet. But I bet police follow him about everywhere. I bet he can't even go to buy a newspaper without them on his tail. Is that what you call exciting?'

'I'm going anyway.' Tim was sulking now.

'And what makes you think *he*'ll let you?' Sue nodded at Crasner. 'Even supposing Dad wanted you with him in the first place?'

The suggestion that he might not was enough.

67

Tim leapt across the table to punch Sue. He missed, lost his balance and fell, sprawling across the table. A vase of flowers was knocked off the table and crashed to the floor. Sue was shocked but she tried to help Tim up. Tim didn't want her help. Anger still surged through him. Some of that anger belonged to how he felt about his father but he wasn't here yet and Sue was, so he took it out on her.

He grabbed her long hair and pulled. She screamed and hit back in self-defence which only made Tim pull harder.

It was Crasner who separated them. He forced open Tim's hand then picked him up and dumped him back in his chair with such force that Tim and that chair overbalanced so that he crashed to the floor.

'Put your hands up!'

It was Sue who spoke. To get Tim off her and to stop the racket, he'd put the gun on the table. In the split second during which he'd been dumping Tim back in his chair she'd seen her chance and grabbed the gun.

'I said, put your hands up!'

10

'Don't move, I mean it!' Sue stood up and moved behind her chair to get a little distance between herself and Crasner.

Tim, still rubbing himself after his fall, began to move round the back of Crasner to join Sue.

'Stay where you are, Tim.'

He froze. 'What do you mean? I'm on your side!'

'Are you?' She was holding the gun out in front of her. It needed two hands and even then she couldn't keep it steady but her voice was very still. 'I'd like to believe you but I can't.'

Tim looked at his feet. He knew exactly what she meant. He wasn't even sure himself whose side he was on. He loved his sister, in spite of the heated argument they'd just had. He didn't like Crasner one bit. But what was worse he knew that they would both, for their different reasons, try to prevent him leaving with Dad.

Tim looked at the clock on the wall. It was ten past five. Dad must have been delayed but he'd be here any minute. Now that Sue had the gun what would she do when Dad knocked on the door? Tim wished that he'd been the one to get his hands on the gun. He'd have known what to do all right – wouldn't he?

'That thing's loaded, kid!'

'I hope so, otherwise you've been making fools of us.'

'It's got a hair trigger.' Crasner was looking really worried now. Sweat was pouring down his face.

'Then you'd better keep still.'

'OK, OK.' Crasner waved both hands in front of his face as if he was trying to push Sue further away.

Tim kept looking from one to the other, not knowing which side to be on or what to do. He knew in his heart he should have been helping Sue, but the thought of running away to Spain with his dad was too good to let go.

Sue's hands were shaking even more now. Partly from holding the gun out in front of her for so long but also from nerves. Having got this far, she didn't know what she was going to do next. She wanted to get Tim and herself out of the house without Crasner. Half an hour ago that would have been easy enough but not since Tim had got this crazy idea into his head about running away. Now she didn't think she could trust him. The alternative was to go alone. But that was unthinkable. However stupid her brother was being she couldn't leave him with Crasner.

71

Maybe she could make it to the phone? Ring for the police. The only trouble was Crasner and Tim stood between her and the door to the hall.

'Why don't you just put the gun down on the table before you have an accident?' Crasner's voice was dry and tense. He was trying to sound reasonable.

'No,' Tim said quickly, 'don't do that!'

Sue couldn't help smiling a little in spite of how nervous she felt but it came out twisted. 'You don't trust him either, do you, Tim?' Tim shook his head.

'All right,' shouted Crasner, 'don't put it on the table but for God's sake stop pointing it at me!'

'You'd didn't mind so much when it was the other way round,' Sue pointed out. The gun was pointing at Crasner's feet but she lifted it. Crasner thought she might shoot so he ducked sideways.

Sue thought he was diving at her. As she stepped back her finger squeezed the trigger very slightly but just enough. There was a loud explosion. Sue dropped the gun. Tim and Crasner hit the floor at the same second as the glass from the broken window showered down.

In the confusion Sue thought she'd hit one of them and was terrified it might be Tim. Tim, who wasn't hurt, wondered if she'd got Crasner.

But Crasner was getting up to his feet and the gun was back in his hand.

Somewhere out across the gardens a dog was barking. It was the only sound they could hear apart from Crasner breathing heavily.

'Right!' snapped Crasner. 'That's enough tricks. Get back on those seats and this time stay there.' He'd edged away from them as far as possible and was standing with his back up against the sink unit. 'If either one of you moves from now on I'll shoot first and think about it later, understood?'

Tim nodded.

Sue barely acknowledged that he'd spoken. She was shaking from head to foot. She was biting her own finger to stop herself crying out. Her hair had fallen across her face, but Tim could tell that she was crying.

'I'm sorry, Sue,' he said quietly. 'I am on your side against him. It's just that I want to go with Dad. It's part of a dream. I know that may sound stupid but when I thought he was dead I used to lie awake for hours wondering what he was like. Because Mum wouldn't ever talk about him I made up my own stories. Now I've got the chance to find out

73

and I can't just let that chance go. I have to go with him to find out one way or the other. I'll probably come back,' he added, 'but I've got to go. Do you understand?'

Sue, tears rolling down her face, nodded and then brushed the hair back from her face. 'But don't you see he's going to let you down again. Just like he let us all down by running out on us? He *isn't* coming!'

'Oh, yes, he is,' said Crasner.

But Sue kept on shaking her head. 'No he's not. Because the money isn't here.'

'You don't know that for sure, kid.'

'Yes, I do. 'When Dad "died" we went to stay at Gran's for a couple of days. I'd forgotten what happened until a moment ago. I remember everything now. When we came back to the house, the whole place looked as though a whirlwind had hit it. Drawers were pulled out, the contents all over the floor. Floorboards were ripped up in places. My bed had been stripped. My favourite teddy bear had been tossed into a corner. That upset me more than all the rest put together. I asked Mum what had happened. She was crying. She said we must have had a burglary.'

'The fuzz. They'd searched the place.'

'Exactly. So if the money had been here they would have found it, wouldn't they?'

'They might have,' Crasner grudingly admitted.

'Believe me, the state the place was in there wasn't a needle left they hadn't seen, let alone two

74

million pounds.' Sue rubbed her face dry with the backs of her hands. 'I think he took it all with him. He never intended you to have your share. Haven't you noticed the time, both of you, it's half-past five. If he was coming he'd be here by now.'

'It's your fault,' hissed Crasner. 'Firing that bloody gun off. You've scared him away.'

'If he was coming in the first place.'

'He promised. He got word back to me where I've been hiding that he was coming.'

'In that case the police probably picked him up the moment he set foot in the country. They must have been tapping his telephone so that they could keep a check on his movements. They'd be waiting to pounce the second he set foot here.'

'Don't talk wet. I didn't use the phone. I got friends to talk to him. They brought a message back. He promised he'd come.' Crasner bit his lip but he couldn't take his eyes away from the seconds ticking away on the kitchen clock.

'He isn't coming. He's let us all down. I knew he would.' She turned to Crasner. 'Shouldn't you be thinking about how you're going to get away? You can't hang around here for ever. Even if nobody heard that shot and phoned for the police you can't hang about on the off-chance. Mum will be back eventually, then you'll have three prisoners to look after.'

Sue was getting back her old confidence again with every word she spoke.

Crasner was worried and Tim was just bitterly disappointed.

'Are you going to go out the way you came in? I mean you can't just walk out of the front door if the police are looking for you, can you?'

'Shut up!' shouted Crasner brandishing the gun at her. 'Just keep that big mouth of yours shut or I'll shut it for you.'

'It just seems a pity to get caught when you've got nothing to gain by staying here any more.'

Tim admired Sue's courage in talking to Crasner this way, but he could also see that Crasner was just about at the end of his tether. Any moment he might snap and anything might happen.

'Just shut up! I can't think with you going on like that. . . .'

The front door bell shut everyone up.

11

'It's Dad!' Tim leapt to his feet, but when Crasner took a step towards him with the gun he sank back into his chair.

'It's more likely to be the police,' said Sue.

'Just keep quiet, the both of you. I've got to think this out.'

Tim was bouncing up and down on his chair. 'If we don't answer the door he'll go away,' he pleaded.

'If it's the police they won't go away, they'll come in and get you.'

'I said, shut it!' Crasner wiped the sweat off his face with the palm of his hand.

'Whichever it is they won't stay on the doorstep for ever,' murmured Sue.

Tim wished she'd shut up almost as much as Crasner did because it only confused Crasner and delayed things even longer. In reality, Tim was so sure that it was his father that he simply wanted to run down the hall, throw open the door and get him inside before anything went wrong.

'It isn't Dad, Tim, you should know that by now.'
The tone in Sue's voice was one of pity.

Crasner blinked his eyes and shook his head as if
to clear out all the rubbish. 'He said he was coming
and he's come.'

'That's right,' Tim urged him on. 'Let's get on
with it.'

Crasner pulled him back. 'We got to be careful,
just in case. Put the lights out in here.'

Tim, his heart thumping against his chest with
excitement, leaped towards the switch and snapped
out the kitchen lights. The contrast was sudden and
it was a few seconds before their eyes adjusted to the
small amount of light which filtered through from
the hall light.

Crasner had backed away into the shadows.
'Right. Now this is what we're going to do. You two
move over to the hall door. When I say, we switch
off the light out in the hall. Is there a light outside
the door?'

'Yes,' said Sue dully.

'Is it switched on?'

'I think so, yes.'

'Right. Tim, you go down the hall and open the
door. Open it wide, all the way and stand clear.
Understand?' Tim, forgetting Crasner could barely
see him, nodded. 'Do you understand?'

'Yes.'

'Right. Now, you,' he turned towards Sue. 'Stay
up this end of the hall just ahead of me. Remember,

Tim, if you try anything funny, she gets is. Got it?'

'Yes. Let's get on with it!'

The doorbell rang again. Longer this time, more insistent.

Crasner moved over behind Sue. 'Get over to the door. Don't switch the light off until we're all together. Then I'll count up to five, Tim, then you go slowly down the hall and open the door.'

Tim shifted his weight anxiously from one foot to the other as he waited for his sister to join him in the doorway.

In the pale light from the hall he tried to read the expression on her face but her eyes were downcast and he couldn't. He just hoped she wasn't going to do anything stupid and spoil everything.

Crasner joined them but stayed a step or so away in case one of them tried to grab the gun. 'OK,' he spoke through clenched teeth, barely even moving his lips, 'switch out the light.'

Tim did as he was told. The second the light went out the porch light projected the figure of a man standing on the doorstep on to the frosted glass panel of the door in black and white like an old film.

Crasner began to count. 'One, two . . .'

Tim wished he wouldn't count so slowly. The figure of his father eased his weight and Tim thought he was going to turn and leave.

'Three, four . . .'

Crasner's voice was flat and regular. Tim watched as his dad stood waiting impatiently, his hands stuffed into the pocket of what looked like an overcoat.

At last Crasner said, 'Five!'

Without waiting to be told, Tim set off down the dark hallway towards the light that fell on to the carpet through the frosted glass. His heart was thumping so loudly he couldn't understand why the others couldn't hear it.

'Slower!' Crasner hissed after him.

Tim slowed down to what felt like slow motion. After what seemed like hours he had his hand on the Yale lock. At that moment Tim wished with all his heart that Mr T, Murdoch or any of the A-Team, even Face, was standing beside him. His courage seemed to be draining away, running out of his body, passed his shaking knees, out through his feet. His grip was almost too weak to twist the lock but at the slightest noise Tim noticed the shoulders of the figure outside stiffen.

'Come on, kid, open the door!' hissed Crasner.

'I'm doing my best,' Tim whispered back.

When the handle of the lock suddenly twisted a push from outside took the door straight out of his hand and Tim was left on the wrong side of the hall.

'Dad!' Tim shouted out as the door crashed into the opposite wall. Then he saw the now familiar glint of light on metal. Dad had a gun.

Crasner must have seen it too. There was a deafening explosion from Crasner's gun. The narrow hall was too small for the sound. It seemed to press the walls outwards. In the same second Tim saw the dark figure go crashing past him into the hall. As it fell, there was another explosion as the other gun went off but this time muffled by the heavy body that had fallen on top of it.

Sue was screaming at the end of the hall. One scream after another. Loud, empty wails like a hurt animal.

Tim felt tears sting his eyes as he dropped to his knees beside the still, unmoving figure that lay full length on the hall carpet, half in and half out of the door.

'Dad! Dad! Say something, Dad.'

Tim knew all about guns. All about cops and

robbers. All about the A-Team and The Dukes of Hazzard. Nobody ever really got hurt in those. You always saw the crooks getting up and being led away at the end of the episode none the worse for their adventure.

But this wasn't like that. He just lay there on the carpet. Dark, heavy and still.

Tim tugged at his arm but although heavy it was limp like a stuffed toy. Frantically, he clutched at the overcoat, tried to roll him ove but he was too heavy. He grabbed at a handful of the overcoat on the back in the centre and felt something wet and sticky. Tim snatched his hand away. In the harsh light from the porch the stain on his hands looked more brown than red but he didn't have to be told that it was blood.

Not the sort of blood you see on films. Real blood from a body that was oozing the stuff.

Tim's face was wet with tears as he screamed down the hall at Crasner, 'You've killed him! You killed my dad!' Then he buried his face in the overcoat and sobbed so that his tears mingled with winter drizzle and blood.

Tim didn't care about anything any more. 'You've killed my dad!' He repeated it over and over again until he felt hands on his shoulders.

Angrily he shrugged them away.

'It's me, Sue. Crasner's gone.'

Tim turned and fell into her arms. 'He's killed Dad,' Tim sobbed.

'Tim, this man's got red hair, it isn't Dad.'
As Tim turned to look, the shadow of a policeman
fell across them.

12

The blue flashing lights of the police cars and the ambulance had gone hours ago. The street outside was deserted and even Mrs Howson who had rung the police, had reluctantly allowed her curtains to flap back into position. To all appearances, everything was back to normal, but Tim didn't believe that anything would feel normal ever again. The whole house felt uncomfortable, foreign. It was as if Tim, not Crasner, was the stranger.

He knew that the police had eventually caught Crasner scrambling across the back garden wall. He knew he was back under lock and key in prison. It should have made Tim feel safe again but it didn't.

It was very late at night. Tim lay hunched up on a camp bed in Sue's room. Knowing that Crasner had often spent the night in his room, Tim had refused to sleep there alone. He wasn't sure how long it would be, if ever, before he would be able to sleep in his own room again. Just going in to collect his pyjamas had made his skin creep and he'd done that with the light on.

But it wasn't just his room, every room in the house seemed to bring back the image of Crasner. After the police had gone Sue had decided to take a look at the cellar.

'Come on! You're not scared, are you?'

'Of course not,' Tim said with a shrug, but he was. There was something awful about standing in that dank cellar looking at the great gaping hole Crasner had cratered out of the floor in his desperate search for the money.

But it was just the same sitting in the kitchen talking to the police. Tim couldn't believe he'd ever be able to sit on one of those chairs without remembering how it felt being tied to it.

The police had asked lots of questions. Time after time they'd gone over seemingly simple things to make sure there was no mistake but the police didn't deal with the ideas that most disturbed Tim.

Now he knew that somewhere he had got a father. Tim wasn't sure if he would have been better off not knowing that Dad was still alive because a good many of the things Tim had found out about him were far from pleasant. Even so, he was his father and, in spite of everything that had happened, Tim couldn't help part of him feeling pulled towards him.

The other thing that bothered Tim was Mum telling that lie in the first place. Obviously, she always knew that Dad wasn't dead but she'd deliberately kept that fact from them.

After the police had left, Mum had made some hot chocolate. Nobody felt like eating then and they'd sat round looking at each other like strangers trying to get to know each other all over again.

Mum had said she was sorry about the lie, that she only did it to protect them and it was wrong and she should have told them the truth.

Tim could tell she meant it, but it didn't make the lie go away. It had been told and he was sure he'd never, never be able to believe a grown-up again.

But already he was living a lie. He certainly hadn't told her, the police, or anyone else that he'd had every intention of leaving with his father when he came to collect the money. But the thoughts he had still lived uneasily in the dark corners of Tim's mind.

But Sue knew.

Tim twisted his head round to look at her. The bedside lamp left her in a pool of golden light. Looking at her lying there calmly reading it was difficult to believe that anything unusual had happened to her that day. Tim wondered how she could lie there concentrating on a book when his head was such a turmoil of confused ideas and emotions.

She must have felt his eyes on her for suddenly she glanced up and smiled at Tim. 'Ready for me to put the light out?'

That was the very last thought in Tim's mind.

The idea of the room in total darkness, even with Sue there to share·it, was the most awful thought.

He swallowed deeply before he spoke. 'I'd rather keep it on, if you don't mind.'

She shrugged. 'OK.' She stuffed an old envelope into the book to keep her place then lay down on the pillow and shut her eyes.

Tim was still watching her, his eyes wide open. There was one more thing he had to say before he could even think of going to sleep. He couldn't apologise to her for the way he'd behaved, although in some ways he thought he'd let her down, but he had to say something.

'You were right about Dad not coming.'

Sue kept her eyes closed. 'Mmm.'

'I should have listened to you. I'm sorry.'

'Forget it,' she murmured.

'Sending a hit man to kill Crasner so that he didn't have to share the money was the obvious thing to do, wasn't it?'

Sue opened one eye. 'A what?'

'A hit man. That's what it's called when you pay someone to kill someone else.'

She shut the eye again. 'Go to sleep.'

Tim turned over in bed away from the light and away from Sue. He pressed his cheek into the cool, white pillow but his eyes were still wide open staring at the blank wall. 'Do you think we'll ever see Dad now?'

For a moment Sue didn't answer and Tim thought

she was already asleep. Then she spoke softly. 'What's the point if he doesn't want to see us?'

Tim didn't answer. A single tear rolled down his cheek and made a grey, wet patch on the pillow. It was for a dream which had almost become a reality but had been shattered for ever.

'Go to sleep, Tim. It's Friday tomorrow. It's 'Knight Rider' tomorrow evening,' Sue reminded him, sleepily.

But try as he could Tim found he couldn't get an image of Michael Knight clear in his mind. Instead he kept seeing Crasner. He even thought he could smell the sweat of the man, the sweat of fear.

Then he remembered the sound of the gun going off. The first time, when Susan fired, in the kitchen. The shot that had made somebody ring for the police. And then the second shot that had killed the man in the hall.

He could smell the acrid smell of gunpowder, hear Sue screaming and feel the warm, sticky blood on his fingers. He'd washed his hands several times, scrubbed them with a nail-brush but although there was nothing left to see, the sticky sensation of blood remained.

The other thought that was crystal clear in Tim's mind was the realisation that if Crasner's shot had been just a couple of feet to the right, he was the one who would have been spread out on the hall carpet.

Tim began to shiver under the bedclothes but to his surprise he found he could suppress, control it.

Maybe there was some of his father's toughness in him. Tim knew that only he could decide how best to use it. Although today his dreams had been trampled on, perhaps his grip on reality was strengthening.

13

The ground was iron hard with frost. The last dead leaves clattered across it, driven by the North wind.

Although the cemetery was crowded, not a single relative of the dead man had turned up for the funeral. There were a few ghoulish members of the public who had read about the shooting and the recapture of Crasner. There were also a number of policemen, who'd mainly come to keep order but were there just on the off-chance that Crasner's partner might turn up. But the bulk of the crowd was made up of newspaper reporters and photographers.

Tim and Sue knew nothing about the funeral. Their mother thought they'd been through enough. Tim was still having bad dreams and although Sue didn't say much, it was easy to see how relieved she was when Mum got home from work at night. So Mum hadn't mentioned the subject and she'd gone to work just as usual.

Crasner certainly wasn't there. Nor was there any question of his having an operation and giving him another chance to escape. Instead he'd been moved to a maximum security jail while he waited to face charges of manslaughter.

The most curious thing about the funeral was that it had been paid for anonymously. Had Crasner's partner paid? But despite the best efforts of the press, nobody could prove anything one way or the other.

The brief graveside service was coming to an end. The coffin was lowered into the ground, not to silence but to the accompaniment of the shutter clicks and motorized whirrings of the press cameras. The flashes zapped through the cold, grey light of the winter's day like forks of lightning. Only the press photographers were sorry to see the last of the coffin.

The members of the public who'd been watching had turned their backs almost before the gravediggers had sent the first spadefuls of frozen earth thudding down on its lid. The policemen beat their black, gloved hands together while the pressmen sped off to meet their deadlines.

As the last people made their way past the rusting, wrought-iron gates of the cemetery, fine snow began to fall, gently dusting the ground white. It was like watching someone grow old before your eyes.

Beside a swimming pool in Southern Spain a lithe, tanned man with tousled, blonde hair was sipping a pink drink. Lumps of ice chinked against the glass. Despite the heat of the sun he suddenly shivered.

For some reason some words his father used to say to him flashed into his mind. 'Do as you would be done by.' Somewhere deep in his gut he had an awful feeling they might prove to be only too true.

Until that moment he hadn't given the funeral a second's thought.